THIS BOOK BELONGS TO:

_____

To the community who has walked with us these last four years,
finding Jesus on every page and everywhere along the way.
When we count up our friends, you are some of our very best.
—EBF and DB

For Papa, the seeker and storyteller.
—SJW

Text © 2022 Emily Belle Freeman, LC, and David Butler
Illustrations © 2022 Sarah Jane Wright

Visit us at deseretbook.com

Library of Congress Cataloging-in-Publication Data
(CIP data on file)
ISBN 978-1-63993-068-5

Printed in China
RR Donnelley, Dongguan, China   5/2022
10 9 8 7 6 5 4 3 2 1

More Than Just a Star

EMILY BELLE FREEMAN and DAVID BUTLER

Illustrated by SARAH JANE WRIGHT

DESERET BOOK

"Micah, it's time for sleep."

It was long past bedtime, but the shepherd boy still lay awake under the starry sky.

"Papa," said Micah, "what should I dream about?"

"Dream about the Messiah, the One who is coming. One worth watching for."

"But Papa," the young boy replied, "how will I know what to watch for?"

"The prophecies say that when the Messiah comes, there will be a new star, brighter than the rest," his father answered. "This will help you remember."

"But you are watching for more than just a star."

Early the next morning, Micah and his father started the walk into town. On his shepherd's flute, Micah's father played a melody full of joy and peace. It reminded Micah how his heart had felt when his father told him about the Messiah the night before.

"Papa, tell me again, what should I watch for?"

"Watch for heavenly messengers who will bring good tidings and a promise of peace, angels who will lift up their voices together and sing."

As they neared the city, Micah's father handed him the flute to put in his bag for safekeeping.

"But don't forget, you are watching for more than just a song."

It wasn't long before they reached the edge of town. The small market within the city of Bethlehem was busier than usual because so many people were coming to be taxed.

"Papa, will you tell me another prophecy?" the young shepherd boy asked.

"The Messiah will come from Bethlehem," said Father, "even though some call it the least, the smallest of Judah."

He pulled out a few coins to buy Micah a special Jewish fruit from a cart nearby, a small red pomegranate—one of Micah's favorite treats.

"This is to remind you that our Messiah will come from this place, though it be little. His story will begin here."

"But you are watching for more than just one from Bethlehem."

As his father finished his shopping, Micah watched a wealthy man purchasing frankincense from a stall nearby. The shopkeeper filled a bag to overflowing.

Noticing the boy's interest, the rich man walked over and placed one piece of the costly incense in Micah's bag as a gift.

"Watch for kings who shall bring gifts," Micah's father said to the boy.
"But you should be watching for more than just a gift."

As they left the city, Micah and his father
saw a group of Roman soldiers.

Micah's father said, "It will not always
be like this. One day the Messiah will
come to make us free."

"What will He be like?" asked the boy.
"He will be a prince of peace."

"This is a symbol of peace," his father said, handing an olive leaf to Micah to place into his bag. "Let it remind you what our prince will bring." Micah could hear the hope in his father's voice as he continued,

"But He will be more than just a prince."

Once they were back with their flock, Micah helped his father shear one of their lambs.

Micah asked quietly, "Papa, how else will I know Him when he comes?"

"Watch for a shepherd who feeds His flock and gathers His lambs," said Father. "One who carries them when needed and gently leads them along."

Papa handed a small handful of wool to Micah.
"Keep this in your bag to remind you," he said.

"But remember, He will be more than just a shepherd."

The boy sat down in the tall grass as his father went to work repairing the rock wall that protected the sheep.

"The Messiah will be known as a rock and a fortress.

"If you add this to your bag of treasures," his father said, "it will help you know how to recognize Him."

"But remember, He will be more than just a rock."

That afternoon Micah settled next to the stream as his father guided the sheep near the water.

"Papa, what else do the prophecies tell us?" the young boy asked.

"There will be One who leads His sheep to still waters. A protector who brings comfort through the safety of His staff," the father replied.

"But He will be more than just a staff of protection."

Walking alongside the sheep as they grazed, Micah tripped
on the uneven ground and skinned his knee.

His father pulled a vial of oil out of his shepherd's pouch and began to gently clean the wound with cloth.

"Watch for One sent to people like us, the needy, the poor, those with no helper. Watch for One who will come to bind the broken hearts. To comfort those that mourn," his father said.

"He will bring the oil of joy for mourning."

"But He will be more than just the oil of joy."

After supper, Micah opened his bag and poured out all of his treasures. He held each one carefully and tried to remember each of the prophecies his father had taught him.

"Tell me again, Papa, what will the Messiah be like?"

"Watch for a light that will shine through the darkness."
His father reached into a basket nearby and pulled out an unlit oil lamp
for Micah to keep in his shepherd bag.

"But remember," he whispered as they fell asleep,
"He will be more than just a light."

In the darkest hours of the night, Micah awoke.
"Come quickly, it's time," his father urged.
In the distance Micah heard the call of a mother sheep.
A baby was coming.

It was a firstborn. If the lamb was completely white,
they would swaddle it to keep it safe for the temple.

"Watch for a lamb without spot," his father said softly as he gently wrapped the lamb in swaddling cloth. "One born for sacrifice."

The father handed Micah a small piece of cloth. Micah held the piece next to his heart for a moment, considering the words he knew his father was thinking—

He will be more than just a lamb.

Suddenly, Micah and his father looked up and heard a choir
of angels in the midst of heaven singing the long-awaited song.
Micah saw a new star shining over the little town.

"Papa, is this what we have been waiting for?" Micah asked breathlessly.

"Come, it is time!" His father began to run.

"Papa, what should I watch for?" the shepherd boy asked as he ran.

"A tiny baby!" The boy could hear the excitement and anticipation in his father's voice.

"They will call His name Immanuel," he continued as they ran toward the city.

Their steps slowed as they
neared the stable. "Remember,"
Micah's father whispered,
"He will be more than just a baby."
Micah clutched his treasures
close and believed.

He knew this baby would be . . .

More than just a star
More than just a song
More than just one from Bethlehem
More than just a gift
More than just a prince
More than just a shepherd
More than just a rock
More than just a staff of protection
More than just the oil of joy
More than just a light
More than just a lamb

He reached down and took a piece of straw and placed it in his bag to remember.

Baby Jesus would be all of these.

The Messiah.
Immanuel.
God with us, in each of our stories.

Everything he hoped for.

And more.

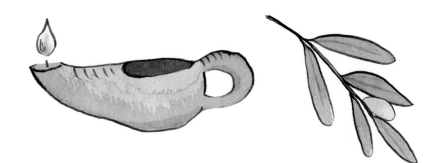

PROPHECY	SYMBOL	REFERENCE
a new star	star	Numbers 24:17
good tidings	flute	Isaiah 40:9
come out of Bethlehem	pomegranate	Micah 5:2
offering of gifts	frankincense	Psalm 72:10
prince of peace	olive leaf	Isaiah 9:6
shepherd	wool	Isaiah 40:11
fortress and strength	rock	2 Samuel 22:2; Psalm 18:2
one who protects	staff	Psalm 23
oil of joy	oil	Isaiah 61:3
light	lamp	Psalm 18:28
spotless lamb	lamb	Numbers 28:3
a baby, Immanuel	straw	Isaiah 7:14